The Art of Otherness

Presents

MU CHALO

Migrant life stories inspired by Bemba proverbs

MAYASE JERE

Stories by MAYASE JERE

Illustrations by AMANDA MUTHIKE GATENDE

Published in 2023 by Olana's World Publishing House
Olana's World Publishing House
Melbourne Australia
https://agnesnsofwa.com.au/

ISBN 978-0-6454134-5-8 (Paperback)

ASIN B0C587R1J4 (ebook)

For Mummy Leah and my Bemba mothers watching over me:
Ba Mbuya, Big Mummy, Mummy Ives, Mummy Joan

Maswaswa made it!

ABOUT THESE STORIES

Author, Mayase Jere, brings Zambian Bemba proverbs to life through stories of migrant journeys. Her early childhood was spent with her grandmother who loved using Bemba proverbs to chastise her. Some days, she feels as though she is losing her grandmother's teachings. These stories, inspired by the proverbs, are Mayase's way of remembering her roots and sharing Bemba with the world.

The stories may be fictional but they include highly emotional, disturbing, and at times light-hearted incidents that Mayase, her friends, and many others who have migrated from their home countries, experienced.

The common theme is everyone's migrant journey is unique – particularly here in Australia. Some are similar, but with a different set of troubles, sorrows, financial stresses, and happiness sprinkled here and there.

INTRODUCTION

Mayase's book, Mu Chalo, brings Bemba Proverbs to life (her words), and magically provides a window into the 'in between' world of her birthplace in Zambia, and migrant life here in Australia: the fears of deportation; the trials of menial employment; the wisdom she attained through her 'Bemba mothers'; but ultimately, i#t is the dream of a western education, and better life, that carries us through this magical book. And although she says it is a work of fiction, the autobiographical radiates from every line.

It is not only her wisdom, but Mayase's positive and honest attitude towards life that emanates from the page, and I feel this is what will be of the greatest value to you the reader. It certainly was for me. It is a book not only for migrants, but for those wishing to understand the challenges and courage it takes to pack one's bags and leave behind everything you have ever known. To read this book is to understand Mayase's world: a world of hope and beauty, and at times, painfully experienced.

"If I cut her, will she bleed?" says a young boy to his mother in a supermarket, in 1980s Scotland. Big Mumma snatches her hand back in horror. These words will be remembered for generations, and perhaps generations more now they have found their way into this book. Whether they were uttered in innocence or maliciousness, is not relevant. They exemplify the trials faced by migrant women – and men (who narrate some stories) – and the onion-like layers of intersectionality that is a persistent barrier to the full life potentially lived.

Richard Dove
Author of Us Karen & The Promise

Contents

PART I

Umubala Kale, Ulayafwilisha

An Early Beginning Is Half the Battle

Ketiwe was running late again. But she was not leaving the house without a cup of tea. Clutching her red keep-cup, the kitchen filled with rooibos aroma. Suddenly, she was transported back to Chilenje South Seventh Day Adventist church youth camp in Kafue. This was happening a lot these days: ruminating about her childhood in her Melbourne home. Feeling like she belonged there, but knowing she didn't. The sensation of being happy and sad at the same time.

Church youth camp was a recipe for mischief. The teenagers were excited to be away from their parent's watchful eyes. The supervisors were young adults in their early 20s, trying to prove their adulthood. Ketiwe and her friends loved the freedom the camp provided. They got to wander the vnwoods during that week in the bush. They loathed the pretend holiness. If it were up to them, the church service would not be part of the program at all.

The camp was like a tele-novella. Sneaky relationships. Gossip. And a healthy dose of jealousy. There were nights filled with star gazing, games, and whispers of snakes in the camp area. Not to mention the fights in the bushes over a crush that was no longer secret.

For Ketiwe, the best parts were hiking up mountains, and bathing in cold streams. There was a simplicity out there that the crowded city life did not offer. After the first day, the teenagers forgot about sulking and not having any hot water to bathe in. It was the perfect place to be part of the land; to appreciate sleeping outside, and kissing boys in the comfort of the moonlight.

The last youth camp she attended swiftly entered her mind. Even *she* didn't know it would be her last with this particular group of church friends. Since this time, she has lost contact with all of them, except Dorcas who is a Facebook "Happy Birthday" friend.

Dragging their suitcases along the gravel roads which led them back to their homes, Dorcas' pretentiousness gave out, "This will be us, going in and out of airports after high school". Neither of them had ever been on an aeroplane. Buses to the village were all they knew. But Dorcas loved to dream, and this gave Ketiwe a chance to imagine a life away from the dust of gravel roads. She didn't know which particular airports she would visit, but she knew she would love that life.

The two girls were showing off, as they always did. They had realised a long time ago that to get the boys' attention - to strike out their competition - they had to be more "western" than everyone else.

From her Facebook posts, Dorcas hadn't lost any of her pretentiousness. But who could blame her, given her family now reside in Dubai. Taking a sip of her rooibos, envy filled Ketiwe's mouth, as the heat stung her lips. Her close childhood friend had it all: the lifestyle, kids and a husband. While Ketiwe was still single, being passed for every promotion, and chasing the dream down under.

Dragging suitcases in Chilenje's red soil, and being critical of others whose suitcases did not have wheels, and instead had to carry bags on their heads, the two girls never imagined their words would come to life. Taking another sip, Ketiwe's envy subsided a little to gratefulness. Because those gravel roads are still there, reminding her of how far she had come.

It may have just been boastful words, speculating about the airports she and Dorcas would be going in and out of after high school, but it was these comments which created the dream that brought her to Australia. She was on a mission to thrive in this life down under.

PART II

Bushe Kuti Waipushya Imbwa Ngeifwele Shi

Can You Ask a Dog If It Is Dressed?

Around a dinner table at Corey's parents' home in Essendon.

Corey: "She speaks good English, which is great to hear for a change."

Her:

Her: Rolls eyes eternally. "What do you mean? Everyone in Australia speaks ok English. Maybe not the Queen's English but it's good isn't it?"

Corey's Father: "Well not everyone who comes from where you come from does, you know"

Corey:

Her: "Mr Sinyange, my High School English teacher would be disappointed if my English wasn't good. I was one of his top students! You *do* know we learn in English in most Southern African schools. Right?" A left eyebrow raises.

Corey:

The first few times Corey commented on her English being "good" she had humbly replied, "Thanks." But since he made it a point to tell his family she spoke "good English," she figured this SNL skit was over, and it was time to set things right.

Her: "Has anyone here actually *been* to Africa?" She looks into each of their eyes, in turn. "Or better yet, *know* anything about Zambia? Huh?"

Corey and Parents:

She suddenly felt sick just as the pavlova arrived. It's exhausting educating these wilful ignoramuses.

Her:

PART III

Inganda Ushilalamo Baikumbwa Umutenge

You Admire the Roof of The
House You Don't Live In

Zuri: "Heysh be serious, this will be a popular podcast one day".

They all laughed. No one believed her. After enjoying her food, the least they could do was indulge her by adding their voices to her recording. They refused to believe their stories were relevant enough to be heard by millions one day. Zuri had no doubt. They just thought she needed this outlet. To pacify her, they quietened, and she began her interview – writing and recording at the same time.

Zuri: Che, what brought you to this country?

Che: "I had no choice. My father's friend had a child in Australia, so when I completed high school I was dispatched here. As the firstborn, I was the example my younger siblings would follow. My father made sure I understood my obligations."

Zuri: And Jelena, what about you?

Jelena: "When I was ten years old, I pointed at Australia on a world map and told my mother I wanted to live there. I knew nothing of the country – I don't think I'd even heard of it. As a young girl, I was fascinated with how far it was. It seemed like the end of the world from Serbia. Who knew a war would break out a few years later and this would bring me to Australia?"

Zuri: Che, what was your biggest challenge migrating?

Che: "Being a man in this place is hard." He looks around for consensus, smiling. "I had to do *everything* by myself – the cooking."

Laughter breaks out.

Zuri: "Ooh, the poor man had to boil his own water. What a shame!"

More laughter.

Che: Looking offended. "Yeah! Yeah ok, do you want me to go on or what?"

Zuri: Smiles. "Please continue, good sir"

Che: "My mother taught me well, but *heysh*! planning your meals and cooking every day is a chore. Those Maccas burgers are too easy! And don't get me started on the women. You can get swept away in the lust of the vast number of ladies that are attracted to a black man." He looks around for laughter. Nobody laughs. "Sometimes you can't tell whether they like you, or it's a fetish trap. But now that I have only eyes for Zuri, wink, wink, I am good…"

Zuri takes a deep breath and turns to Jelena.

Jelena: "I didn't speak any English. I went to language school for one year before university. Luckily, I picked up the language quickly, but on the first day of classes, I could not understand anything my lecturer was saying. I could hear he was speaking English, but I could not comprehend what was being talked about. He was talking too fast. I realised that this was how people spoke English normally. Nothing like the language school speak, which was, 'Heelllooo Jelena." She draws out her words. "Hoow arree you todayyy'?"

Everyone laughs and nods.

"My writing took a lot of time, and I got scared because I couldn't write simple sentences. How was I going to write assignments and essays? I questioned whether I was doing the right thing by pursuing further studies. I paid someone to proofread my work, because I didn't trust myself. Throughout my first year, I thought of quitting many times. My mantra was, *if it wasn't difficult, it wouldn't make you grow;"* The other one was, *"it won't be like this forever. It will get easier. Push through!"*

"I compared myself to native English speakers. If it was easy for them, why not me? I had to constantly remind myself not to compare myself to them and set my own standards. I started enjoying university in my third year. In retrospect, I wish I talked to my lecturers and told them about my struggles."

"I will always speak English with a not-so-Aussie accent. Some people have their opinions about how Aussie you are from that. I don't take that in a bad way. It's their own lack of understanding. It's not an offence to me. It's harder for them than me, I guess."

Zuri: What is your most memorable moment thus far?

Che: "When I landed here at 20, I didn't know what I wanted in life, individually or academically. I just knew I had to get a degree and not disappoint my father. Completing my Master's and hearing the joy in my father's voice when I graduated was a moment I will never forget. He did ask me to do a PhD for him. I laughed it off and said I will see, knowing I never wanted to study ever again."

Zuri: What about you, Jelena?

Jelena: "My childhood best friend and goddaughters came to Australia some years back. They were rejected the first time they applied for their visas. I then put myself as the sponsor for their trip. While studying, I collected funds from the Serbian community to get them over here. It was an amazing feeling seeing how hopeful they were, and remembering how I felt when I arrived. Through their eyes, I saw the belief in a better future. After living in a refugee camp for 10 years, being reunited with your loved ones, and seeing a brighter future, is priceless."

Zuri: What wisdom would you like to share with those migrating from their homelands?

Che: "You will clean poop and that's ok. If you keep going and don't stop, the time will pass quickly."

Jelena: "Leave the past in the past. Do not get caught up in comparing your new home to your motherland. You will never have what you had at home. Remove the expectations of how people should or shouldn't be. Most things will be different. Embrace that. See the best in people."

Zuri: What were you told about Australia that turned out to be untrue when you arrived?

Che: "Life is easy overseas. At some point, I was having less than four hours of sleep per night holding down three or four jobs."

Jelena: "I was told Melbourne had the worst weather in the world. Someone said, don't go there, it rains all the time. No sun and very windy. I listened with a pinch of salt. I figured the weather would not be miserable all the time. My mother almost changed her mind because of the weather."

Zuri: What do you love the most about Australia?

Che: "The salaries. You won't get paid like this back home. You can work as a cleaner and still earn enough to have a good life."

Jelena: "Too many things to mention. There are no barriers to what you can be."

Zuri: What things are Australians most ignorant about regarding your country of birth?

Che: "I was asked a few times whether I am happy to be wearing clothes. Am not sure what Nat Geo is showing people nowadays. Africans *do* wear clothes."

Jelena: "I dislike generalisations. I have found that most people are interested in what is going on in the world. They are interested in knowing more about the world and ask me about my homeland."

Zuri: What is your identity?

Che: "I was told not to forget my roots. I consider myself a grafted apple and lemon tree. My roots are intact, but nowadays my fruit is different and rare. Being Australian doesn't mean you lose your authentic-ness and put your roots into question."

Jelena: "I have kept my accent. My English is a lot clearer now. I speak the best way I can, and I'm a proud Serbian Australian. From the language and cuisine, I have added things I need and removed those that I don't. I have created my own identity that is perfect for who I am."

Zuri: Alright, one more question. What are you most proud of in your journey thus far?

Che: "I came here to make my father proud. To be what he wanted me to be. I think I have achieved that. I am not where I need to be career-wise, but where I am has given me focus on who I want to be. I now have ownership of my journey, and not the expectations of my parents to be a doctor – but I'm working it out. I have built a new family that is filled with friends I have made over the years. It's not your usual "blood family," but it's the family I choose."

Jelena: "The support from the community has been overwhelming at times. I have learnt to be accepting of everyone in this country, and not do things that jeopardise different opinions, cultures and the law. My hubby and little family are also a great achievement! See, I even use the word hubby."

Zuri: No worries, mate!

Laughter breaks out.

Zuri: Ok friends that's a wrap. Who wants dessert?

PART IV

Ubushiku Usheme Nechimbala Chilocha

On A Bad Day, Cold Nshima Will Burn You

Today is what they call bad mashamo. Mashamo means bad luck. The repeated negative intensifies the tragedy that will befall you. If I had known that bad mashamo had attached itself to me, I wouldn't have left the house.

Stuck in this industrial refrigerator, I try to keep my eyes open, wondering whether the $150 I am supposed to make for this shift is worth it. When the agency called offering a 4:00am shift packing food for aged care homes, I thought, why not? I need every dollar I can get to pay those tuition fees. I figured all I needed was about 3 hours of sleep once I'd knocked off at midnight from my office cleaning gig. With the early start, I will be done in time to catch my evening class.

The cold room felt like it was minus 20 degrees. The warm clothes I had on, including the overalls and gloves – standard issue – you could compare with wearing a t-shirt, walking down the street on a cold winter's morning. My teeth were chattering. The clenching of my jaw was beginning to cause a headache. We were advised to go out and warm our bodies in the heated room next door every 45 minutes.

As the packing was winding down, Mick asked me to start my cleaning duties. The dishes needed washing, the floor required sweeping and mopping, the benches cleared, and everything packed away on the metal shelves. Finally, everything looked tidy enough for me to head home. As I approached the door to warmth, Mick yelled "Mate! Did you clean the freezer?"

"Freezer," I repeated. "Were we not in the freezer?" I wondered.

"Yes, the door next to the exit sign," Mick insisted. "Mate. you can't go without finishing the cleaning!"

I turned my eyes slowly away from his. I knew I was not going to get paid for whatever extra time I would spend in there. I hadn't noticed the freezer. If the cool room we had spent all day in was the European winter, then the freezer was Antarctic winter. I could barely hold the cloth to wipe the metal shelves. Taking a deep breath, I heard Mick shout through the slightly opened door, "Hurry up, mate! I need to pick up my daughter at 3pm!"

Dragging the mop methodologically left to right, following the floor pattern so as not to leave diagonal trails, I walked backwards towards the door so my steel cap boots did not leave footprints on the freshly washed floor. A sigh of relief escaped my shivering lips when my heel touched the door. Finally, I could get out of here. Grasping the doorknob, my hand slipped a few times. Come on now Antarctic freezer door, I said to myself, I am not going to lose my fingers opening you without gloves. Come on hands, we need the warmth of the heaters. After a few tries, I realised it was not the gloves or my hands failing their duty. The doorknob was not turning. My clenched teeth began to chatter with fear. Using both hands, I tugged at the door knob. There was no movement up or down. I began banging hard upon the metal door, as it struck me that everyone would have left the cool room by now. Mick's office was miles away. No one could hear me scream.

Manic cries for my mother escaped my lips. "Mayo! Mayo!" How could she hear me all the way in Zambia? Moving back a few steps, I lunged forward, slipping before I could press my body against the door. Ouch! My elbow hurt as I clawed back up. I swung my body towards the door. The steel frame pushed me back with a force and knocked my shoulder out of its socket. Ouch! My shoulder and elbow were not the only things causing me pain. My whole body was aching. It was becoming hard to breathe and my voice was gone.

My mother suddenly appeared before me. "Mayo! I didn't think you would hear me!"

"Sonny, I am so proud of you," she whispered, holding my head upon her chest. "You are my favourite child"

A smile stretched through my frozen lips. "You love me more than Ben, right?"

"Sonny, am so proud of you."

It brought me immediate satisfaction. I had bested my big brother Ben, the golden boy of the family.

PART V

Ichi Kwanka Bachimwena Kuma Mpalanya

You Can See the One Who Will Catch You from Their Outstretched Hands

Sitting on the bus, taking Route 75, from what felt like a 24-hour housekeeping shift, she struggled to keep her eyelids open. Having just dozed off, she was suddenly jilted awake with the fear of having missed her stop. She hated walking alone in the dark after these midnight-ending shifts. Groggily, staring straight into a man's disapproving look, she looked behind with the feeling that he was disapproving of something that was happening behind her – but there was nobody there. That feeling she felt quite often nowadays, struggled to be released. Pushing it down, she smiled and looked out the window, praying he was not getting off at her stop.

Walking the low-lit streets that led to her student unit, Big Mummy came into her mind. Her mother's sisters, by tradition, were considered her mothers too. The elder sisters commanded at times even more respect than her biological mother. Big Mummy was the firstborn among her mum's eight siblings. She possessed this calm aura that none of the other mothers had. Maybe they called her Big Mummy because she was the tallest of the five sisters. Or perhaps it was because she was the eldest. She couldn't remember how she and her cousins began calling her Big Mummy. From memory, as a child, they called her ba mummy Bana Chanda, which meant, "mother of Chanda". When all the five sisters were together, if she said mum, all of them responded at the same time. She had to specify which mum she was after.

Big Mummy was her favourite. Her calm demeanour was very similar to her own. She remembered a story Big Mummy often told. It was the 80s, and she was an international student in Scotland studying Nutrition. While out shopping one day, a young boy with brown hair almost covering his curious blues eyes was looking at her. A showdown of stares and smiles ensued. The child's mother, finding it awkward, yanked the young boy's arm. "Stop that!" she chided.

Ignoring his mother, the child whisked free, walked over to Big Mummy. "Can I touch you?" he asked. She indulged the child by holding out her hand. He ran his tiny fingers over her hand, then turned to his mother – whose eyes seemed more angry than apologetic, "Mum, if we cut her, will she bleed?"

Big Mummy snatched her hand away. Glances of embarrassment were exchanged, as the mother dragged the boy away.

Everyone in the family has their own vivid imaginations about what exactly happened in that grocery store that day, and how each of them would have reacted. Older Charmaine thinks she would have chastised the mother. But then she remembered how she reacted to the man on the bus, and now thinks she would most likely have pulled her hand away after the boy finished running his blade through it.

When she got her visa to study in Australia in 2003, she imagined a different world for herself. As she packed her suitcases for Australia, she made a mental note to avoid children in grocery stores. She didn't ever want to be in the same situation as Big Mummy. Big Mummy's 1980s Scotland – a land that saw very few people of African heritage – and 2004 Australia, were practically the same place. 2004 Australia might have had more people of African heritage than 1980s Scotland, but it felt like the adults here were actually scarier than children.

A sigh of relief overwhelmed her as she opened the door to her unit. She wished Big Mummy was there to help her through those stares.

She was too young when the story was told to fully understand what otherness felt like. In this land down under, who would watch over her? Who would come to her aid when those stares turned into punches? She wondered.

PART VI

Kwenda Babili Temwenso

Two People Walking Together Removes Fear

They called each other Bolingo.

Ever since the day they met each other at the city-bound bus stop, they knew love was the only thing that could describe their relationship. It's not that they were inseparable, it was the telepathy: they could sense each other's troubles.

The second Jay answered the phone from "Unknown," he knew there was trouble.

He hadn't heard from Michael in weeks. He assumed the "radio silence" was because there weren't any networks in the middle of the Great Sandy Desert. Michael had gone there to earn his tuition fee. He was promised more weekly pay than the bakery job in the city could offer. The university had threatened him last semester they would report him to the Department of Immigration and Multicultural and Indigenous Affairs (DIMIA) if he did not pay his tuition fees on time.

A week after he left, an email appeared in Michael's inbox, 'Bolingo, hope you are well. I work 18 hours per day. It's great. Call you soon.'

Were those tears he was hearing on the other side of the Unknown number?

Jay: "Bolingo, calm down! What is going on?"

Michael: "I am at a police station. They are moving me to the immigration detention centre in Perth in a few days. Call my dad! Tell him I have been arrested for staying in the country illegally."

The phone cut out before Jay could ask what illegally meant. Or which police station, or detention centre. He had no clue where to start looking. Flipping through the Yellow Pages phone book, his worst fears came to life. He had no clue whether Michael was in the Pilbara or Kimberley regions. Worse than this, no detention centres were listed. How on Earth was he going to help his friend?

Michael was one of those conscientious types, who worked odd hours, putting university first, and chasing girls as a fifth or sixth priority. He took being the first born seriously. It was his duty to ensure his siblings back home had a good education and got the chance, like him, to study abroad someday.

They were an odd pair. Jay was all about the clubs. Ladies' night was Wednesday. Friday, njikata (hold me). Saturday, ndekelako (release me), and the occasional house party on a Sunday afternoon. If he wasn't studying, he was clubbing. His parents sent him money every month and he had no idea how it felt to miss the tuition fees deadline.

Jay pulled himself together, and headed to the local IGA to purchase an international calling card. He had to make that dreaded phone call to Michael's parents. How could this happen to the most hard-working person he knew?

Jay: "Hello, Uncle it's Jabulani. Michael has been arrested and is being transferred to a detention centre for staying in the country illegally."

Uncle: "Ok, let me know when you have more information about what we must do. Thank you for calling, my son. I expected worse."

Michael called two weeks later saying he was at the Perth detention centre near the domestic airport. To this day, Jay shivers, when he thinks of the terror he felt visiting Michael that day. Was DIMIA going to be looking into him as well? Now that he was associated with someone who was getting deported? He wasn't doing too well in his studies.

Is this what an Australian detention centre looks like? He was expecting high electric fences and prison bars. What he found instead felt like a motel with high-security cameras. He was not allowed to carry anything into the centre, especially his phone. It looked more comfortable than he had imagined. There were television screens, an outdoor sitting area and an exercise area. If it wasn't for the gravity of this place, being a detention centre could easily pass for a cheap holiday motel.

Was it weird that their hug lasted longer than usual?

Michael seemed to be looking forward to going home, and getting away from this place. I wondered if it was really true. He said he felt like a weight had been lifted off his shoulders. He was a little annoyed they wouldn't tell him when he was going. Also, they wouldn't let him collect any of his belongings. All he had with him were the clothes he was wearing the day he was arrested.

Michael: "Bolingo. Clear my room and look after my belongings. I will be back for them."

Jay wondered where his optimism came from. He wouldn't be allowed to apply for another visa for at least 3 years. And with a deported tag against your name, who knows if he would be granted a visa in any western country ever again.

Michael's resolve both scared him and gave him hope. He would have his best friend in close proximity soon.

Michael: "Can you believe that after seven years living here, I was one semester away from completing my degree. And now I may have to start again."

Jay: "You could head to China or Malaysia. I hear they have scholarships and universities associated with Australian universities. You could apply for credits for prior study."

Michael: "You know, I had almost raised enough funds for my sister Anita to come. She was so excited to come and join me. I don't know if I can face her."

No words could make it better. They hugged and reminisced of the time Michael worked in a freezer and he almost lost his fingers from frostbite – well not really frostbite, but those freezers at 4am were the worst.

That was the last time they ever saw each other. Michael emailed a few months later to say he would be heading home in two days' time. They would see each other in the motherland someday.

When he got that email, Jay had already started work at the Hyatt Hotel's front desk. It didn't pay much, but it reminded him of the days when he had Michael around, and he felt like he could face anything. He owed it to his friend to finish his studies and not rely on his parent's finances.

PART VII

Ubufumu Buchindika Umwina

If You Respect Yourself
People Will Respect U

Hey, what does Joni Mitchell say in that Janet Jackson song?

Ahh yes, 'Don't it always seem to go... that you don't know what you've got 'til it's gone!'

Yap, that is the whole truth, and nothing but the truth.

We didn't love our ancestors until we could no longer feel their presence. They tried to teach us their ways, but we were focused on RnB, Dancehall butterfly dance moves, chequered shirts around our waists, and bandanas.

It was upon leaving the comforts of the motherland's bosom, that we realised we did not know our traditions. So much wisdom passed on from our ancestors that we never bothered to learn. Who will teach us now? They are now gone from the physical realm, and we have no idea how to connect with them.

We have succeeded in crossing oceans, and after indulging ourselves in all things western, we have come to the realisation that a part of us is missing.

Can you believe it? We actually miss kneeling before our elders; this way of showing respect. Yes in those days we questioned the practice and called it outdated, but now we crave that humility.

All those aunts and uncles who are "not blood" – whose names we do not know – we want them back! We are tired of calling elders, Sally and Harry.

We once desired to speak English all the time. But now we yearn for just a few hours of Tonga or Swahili. We consider ourselves lucky when our children say hello in our language. How aggravating that they will never know the sweetness of our mother tongues.

It is probably another reason the ancestors can't hear us. Do they understand English?

We ponder whether Nyami Nyami – the Tonga god – who has protected and sustained us in difficult times can hear our cries from across the Indian Ocean. We are so far away from the Zambezi River, our ululations cannot fly over the wide, blue ocean.

But then again, he might not hear us, because we have turned our hearts to the Christian God. We do not pour opaque beer on ancestral trees for blessings anymore.

We call ourselves George, instead of Jabulani. Martha instead of Nkosazana. I mean, if the barista cannot spell or pronounce your name, then a whole day can be ruined - because who can live without caffeine? The local coffee world does not appreciate our botanical names – so this is lost too! Queen Elizabeth II had no one in her lineage named Jabulani, but plenty of Georges – so here we are!

Maybe the ancestors can see that we have lost pride in them, and therefore, ourselves.

They ask us, 'How will they respect you when you constantly trade your roots for the comforts of cultural assimilation?'

We cannot answer.

PART VIII

Ichalo Lifupa Kukolokotakofye Waya

Life Is a Bone Chew Your Part and Leave

Standing at the door, trying to get the attention of the nail technician, is like trying to get the waiter to come your way. They never see you no matter how much you stare at them.

The women – I think Vietnamese – speak loudly amongst themselves. Then one of them yells, "Yes! What do you want?"

Sheepishly, as if not to disturb the order of things, I mouth, "Shellac. Manicure."

The nail lady responds "Manicure! Yes?"

I nod, and start to walk over to the seat that is being pointed out.

"How long do you think I have to wait?" I ask, passing the yelling lady.

"Over there, please," is the answer I get. Well, it's not like I have any place to be.

You hear the most interesting stories at a "Glam" nail parlour. The white ladies, two rows down, are talking about how Americans found it hard to understand their Aussie accents – as if they were speaking a foreign language.

The nail lady jumps in, and says, "When I go home, people laugh at my Aussie accent too!"

The white women exchange sneaky glances, then one of them says, cheekily, "Oh really! In China, they can't understand you?"

"I am Vietnamese," the nail lady responds, not missing a scuff in her buffing.

"Ahh right. I guess we are all the same," replies one of the white women. A nervous, but curious laughter fills the room.

The nail lady turns to her colleagues and starts into a vibrant, loud conversation in Vietnamese. They laugh. I wonder if they are laughing at the white lady's ignorance. The white lady is a little annoyed. She looks dead straight at the nail lady. "Are you laughing at my large hands?"

"No, no, no! "You got good hands!"

Their male colleague jumps in with a comment in Vietnamese, and they all laugh.

It's amazing to watch their concentration, not skipping a beat, as they buff, cut, sharpen and insert nails. Customer service here means exiting the parlour with the nail colour, shape and design you requested. Nothing more. In this parlour, the nail ladies and gentlemen rule. No one in this place can demand they speak English. Here it is like you have entered Ho Chi Minh city. They only use English to ask for your preferences.

"Choose colour please."

What am I in the mood for? I ponder. A bright rouge? Sky blue, maybe? A wild green?

As soon as those flirty colours lure me in, I snap back to reality. What will people at work think?

Ahh, the joys of being the only black female architect. I pick the light brown that is close to my skin tone. The last thing I need is site managers focusing on the colour of my nails, instead of my words. It was hard enough to be taken seriously with my feminine appeal always covered up. I wear Aline business tops and loose fitting pants with steel cap boots poking out below. No makeup and a perpetual serious face is my mode on construction sites. Gotta fit in with the boys.

"Careful. Don't cut my skin." The last time I was here, my skin started peeling a few days later.

"Yes, Yes. No cut," replies the nail gentleman.

Without missing a beat, he turns to his colleague and continues his conversation, while still cleaning my cuticles. Were they talking about me now? I wonder. Or are they continuing their discussion about the white ladies?

One base, two colours, and one shining coat of nail polish under UV light, later, he says, "All done." Then moves onto the next customer.

I head to the counter. The conversations in Vietnamese continues, and I think, what if I could take some of this confidence with me onto my next construction site visit? Would they accept me for who I am? I was taught not to rock the boat: to not disturb the order of things. But I am just so tired of trying to be one of the boys.

Walking to the car park a lady in blue stops me. "That is a beautiful colour. Where did you get your nails done?"

"Glam nail parlour just around the corner next to Target," I reply.

God damn! Do I have an acrylic nail polish remover at home? Such a shame my $30 nail manicure is only good for one weekend. I can't have the men on the building site commenting on my nails like this lady in blue. Got to be one of the boys somehow.

PART IX

Uwalinga Ukowa Teminina

A Person on A Mission Does Not Stop

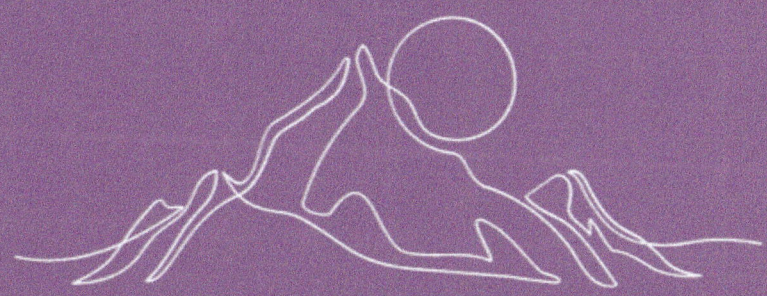

Gone were those sleepless nights she endured while waiting over three years for her permanent residency to be approved. Ten years. Multiple student visas. One bridging visa, and one permanent visa led to this A2 document that was her prized Australian citizenship.

Gone were the days of receiving mail addressed to her from the Department of Immigration and Multicultural Affairs (DIMIA) – which always freaked her out. These dreaded letters always got her heart racing. What had she done wrong? Asked her guilty mind. Had they discovered she worked over the allocated 20 hours per week?

Once, she had opened one such letter to find that all her fears had come true. DIMIA requesting she visit the Immigration office with her letter of enrolment, within 28 days. The terror of it all. Why were they asking?

A few people she knew had recently been deported. Was she to be the next? Her housemates found her in a foetal position, scrunched up on the floor. She didn't hear anything they said. She just handed them the letter up, and mumbled, "What does it mean? Have either of you received this before?"

They both shook their heads, and in their eyes she saw the same terror that was in her soul. One of them said, "Go there with the requested document and it will be fine". She found no solace in her empty words.

The shame and horror of deportation captured her heart. She failed to sleep that night. All she could think about was how close she was to completing her degree. If deported, she would be sent home with a Certificate IV. Not much of a qualification for someone who had been overseas for over five years.

When she got her acceptance letter to study in Australia, her father needed to have enough money in his bank account to cover her tuition fees for eighteen months of College, and four years of University, plus the cost of living expenses, including health insurance. All up, around seventy thousand dollars. This enormous sum needed to be sitting in her father's account for a minimum of three months. He did not have anywhere even close to this!

Her parents borrowed from friends, relatives and high-interest personal loan lenders for them to show that they had the financial stability to support her studies. They even went to the lengths of asking a wealthy friend to use his bank statements, and act as her sponsor. But unfortunately, this fell through when he asked for an exorbitant amount to be part of the lie. This is how things are mu chalo (in the world). Even those who have more than enough are after more money in their pockets.

The immigration office gave her shivers, every time she had to renew her student visa. The financial requirements pain came into play, and she feared being caught out.

This time around coming after being summoned was enough to make her legs fill with lead, but the day arrived soon enough. She grabbed a ticket number and sat down to wait.

"Ticket number 207 head to counter 4" the robotic voice announced as her number flashed on the TV screen. With all the courage she could muster, she walked up to the counter, smiled, and said hello – when really, she felt like bolting out. The lady on the other side just held out her hand for the paperwork. No smile, just a "hello' without looking away from her computer monitor. The immigration officer typed something on her computer, and then looked up sternly.

"Next time, make sure you enrol on time." That was it. Three weeks of sleepless nights for "Enrol on time!"

Her Sherlock mind deduced the university had reported her, when she didn't pay her fees on time. Those bastards! They were not to be trusted. How could they do this to her? Reporting her to DIMIA without even giving her a warning? Was she not a valued student? After all these years paying them thousands of dollars, could they not give her a warning over one simple late payment? Didn't they know she wanted to finish her degree and make her family proud? Didn't it even matter to them at all?

This close encounter made her even more fearful of losing her precious student visa. She told all her fellow international student friends that the university was reporting students who hadn't paid their tuition on time. They had to watch their backs. Deportation was at hand.

Mission accomplished! Holding on tight to that A2 certificate, a deep calm surrounded her. It felt as though, I guess they can't kick me out now! For a long time, it felt like if she breathed the wrong way, her visa would be cancelled. That would be the end of her Australian dream.

But now, a breath of fresh air was upon her. She was finally Australian!

PART X

Ichikalipa Chumfwa Umwine

Pain Is Felt by One's Self

Zuri was accustomed to crying alone. She had forgotten what it was to cry with others.

There was a feeling of camaraderie when sorrow is faced with others: as all yell out together, at the piece that has been ripped prematurely from your lives. This is the way her people mourned at home. Together.

But people here didn't do that. They didn't find comfort in screaming out loud. "Why have you left me?" "Take me too!"

As one throws oneself on the ground, asking their dearly departed why they would leave them in this wretched place, they hear another's voice crying out that same question beside them, and it provides some comfort knowing they are not alone in this pain.

Here in this land, Zuri had no one to scream with. She could not throw herself on the ground and ask why. So she just lay in her cold bed, heart pumping, with an unceasing waterfall of tears, fearing to close her eyes in case something else bad happened.

When she got the call of Che's passing, her first thoughts were, it cannot be. She thought she heard wrong. But was too afraid to ask the person on the other side of the mobile to repeat themselves. Because deep down she had heard clearly; and if they said it again, it would be real. Crumbling to the floor in her work bathroom, she had no recollection of how she got home that day. James encouraged her to be strong, but all she wanted to do was turn into dust, and be nothing. This is what they do not prepare you for when you leave the motherland, she thought. Grieving alone.

Their love died years ago. But his passing removed any residue of hope she had of them ever being together again. Maybe if she had stayed with him, he wouldn't have been with Carrie, dying alone. If she was with him, she would have taken his body home to his ancestors. Instead, Carrie buried him in this land, even before his mother could come to kiss him goodbye.

Zuri was the only black person at his burial. No one talked to her. Maybe they all knew of the time she slashed Che's tyres after she heard he had married Carrie. Her bones screamed "Why? Why have you done this? You have taken our kids to the grave with you. You have taken our future, and left your parents without their only son."

Che's mother arrived a week after the burial, when the family finally put money together for her to travel all the way to Australia from Zimbabwe. Zuri abstained from seeing her. She could not face the woman who could have been her mother-in-love.

Che's family was still fighting with Carrie, to take his body back home to Zimbabwe. Carrie would not allow it. Why are white people so cruel? She thought. Can't she see all they want is for their son to lay with his ancestors? They have lost him already, but to keep him from his ancestors is cruelty his parents will take to their graves.

Friends tell her in comforting words he has gone to a better place. He is with God now. What do they know? Did God himself say he was with him? How could God allow him to die with all her dreams?

Laying there, she dreaded the day she came to this faraway land. All she wanted was to be with her people, yelling, crying, and thrashing on the ground – but that will never happen, because she was there. And Carrie had taken away the man her heart desired.

"I was his wife. Get that through your thick skull!" Carrie had yelled. "He never loved you! If you call here again, I will report you to the police."

But Zuri called again. Begging her to let him rest with his ancestors. And asking why she would let him lie here all alone.

She wants to take back all the terrible things she had said to him in the past. "You will regret this stupid life you are choosing". Well, actually not that one. Because a part of her feels he is regretting seeing the pain Carrie is putting his family through. "What nonsense is this? An African man who just wants to live together, and have children with no lobola? Since when did you become Australian?" she spat at him.

He always had this coy face, that never gave away his anger. "I love you, and we are together. Isn't that what matters? We are not in Zimbabwe anymore."

"What nonsense," Zuri had cried. "It's because your parents did not raise you. That's why you want me and my family to continue living in shame."

She packed her bags that day, believing he would change his mind when she left. But weeks turned into months; months into a year; and then one day, his wedding photo came up on her Facebook timeline – and all of her dreams were lost.

"You are a wicked man for marrying that white woman. After ten years together, all you wanted was a de facto – and then you marry her? God will punish you for this."

Did she cause this? Did God punish him? Because it feels like he is punishing her instead.

She wishes he died never remembering her bitterness.

PART XI

Imiti Ikula Ampanga

The Growing Trees of Today Will Be Forests Tomorrow

"Papa, what is Africa like?"

"Umm, do you mean Bostwana?"

"No. Africa, Papa."

"Well, we are from Botswana *in* Africa, sonny."

I was stalling because I didn't know how to explain the Motherland to my son. How could I explain in a way his five-year-old mind would comprehend?

"I know how to say hello in Setswana. It's Dumela."

"Good job, Amari."

"One day, I will take you to see Nkuku and Ntate mogolo - your grandmother and grandfather."

"In Africa?"

"Yes, Africa. But more specifically Bostwana. It's beautiful there. They have buffalos, lions, leopards, elephants, and hippos – like in your book, Safari."

We haven't been able to travel back to Botswana since the kids came along. And before we knew it, Amari was school age and asking us when he was going to see his Nkuku – not on the phone.

The other day, he came home saying one of his friends said he was from Africa. "Am I African, Papa?"

I didn't know what to say, so I said, "You are Australian and also from Africa." Curious eyes did not comprehend the mambo jambo I was saying. Lucky for me, there was Leggo to distract him. "Look, there's your Leggo set. Build me a giraffe, Amari."

I wondered how to help my son navigate this land. I mean his roots are African, for sure. But he will be more Australian than African when he grows up. Won't he?

Will he still need to convince others that he belongs here? Isn't it enough that he is born, and grew up here? I am hopeful his world will be less focused on where you come from, and that the colour of his skin will not determine his sense of belonging.

When I was younger, walking through the dusty streets of Ikageleng, I longed for the tarred roads I saw on television. People called it "overseas." As I grew accustomed to walking the tarred streets of Perth, I began to long for those dusty Chilenje streets. People called it being "unable to unpack my emotional bags." It was like my body was in this land, but my soul was longing for somewhere else. I missed the noise of the conductors calling out for me to get on the bus, whereas here, the bus drivers pretend they do not see me as they drive away. Apparently, they have to keep time. A few seconds to let on somebody who is practically at the bus door would be too costly.

The stares on Perth buses did not make it easy for me to "unpack those bags" and call "Down Under" home. The clutching of bags close to their chest as I walked past reminded me of the perceived threat I had become. I couldn't understand where it had come from.

Loathing the looks of pity people gave me became the bane of my existence. They had obviously consumed too many World Vision ads. If only they knew that Ikageleng didn't have lions ready to eat you. No thatched huts and no savannah grasslands. It was more like parts of Alice Springs: dusty roads, with red earth.

Some people seemed glad their country pulled me out of my hardship. The only hardship I remember was fighting with bus conductors for change they didn't want to return. All those wars and starvation-riddled World Vision ads made some fear that people like me would bring the war to their quiet neighbourhoods. But the truth is, even *I* fear war as much as *they* do. But my fears were neither seen nor heard.

Looking at Amari, I wondered whether his world will truly be as I hoped. I would hate for his generation to be burdened with the otherness projected by a few wilful ignoramuses who just love pointing out differences. His generation deserves better than to feel the shame associated with the perceived pains of my Motherland.

My wife and I appreciate the power the Australian passport gives us, because we have been through the pain, fear and frustrations of attaining it. This while knowing that western countries maintain the prerogative to refuse you a visa, even though they can enter *your* home country for $50 at the border.

We navigate the third space between the two countries we call home. We are grateful that we have the luxury to study now and pay later. We care that our career options have multiplied. You cannot deny the power of the dollar.

Amari gets to thrive and enjoy the diversity of cultures, as well as the opportunities this country has to offer. More importantly, he has no Motherland bags to "unpack," because calling Australia home is all he knows – for now.

PART XII

Umukulu Apusa Akabwe Tapusa Akebo

An Elder Can Miss a Bull's Eye but Can Never Miss Words of Wisdom

He lay in his bed, wilting away. "Bring the boys to me"

He could feel his last words begin to escape his mind. He felt the sudden urgency that his boys hear his last words.

"They are on their way," someone whispered in his ear. Another voice he couldn't recognise. Probably one of the nurses that tended to his ailing body. It felt like there was a different person each day.

The air in the room got thicker. Sam, the eldest went to lay beside him. John, the middle child knelt on the side of the bed, letting his head fall upon his father's chest. Tom, the youngest lingered at the door.

His father, sensing Tom's hesitation, motioned him to come closer. He shuffled his body next to John, and placed his head upon his father's upper chest, closer to his face. He felt his father's hand cover his head. They lay there in silence; the nurses hushed and left the room.

I lingered at the door, silently weeping. Seeing them all on that bed made me reach for my phone to capture this moment that would most likely be the last with him. His lips started to move, just as I raised my phone. All ears perked, listening keenly.

The time to capture the moment had passed. There would be no picture in the cloud to remind us of this moment. Only what their brains decided to keep; most likely the comfort of their embrace.

I lingered a little longer trying to hear what he was saying, but the message was only for his sons. I could see their heads nodding, and whatever tears had started to fall were gone. I saw a smile start to form around Tom's cheeks as his father pulled him close. Sam's head was covered with his father's hands.

"You are my pride and joy. I leave this earth knowing you will look after the family better than I did.

I bless you with thousands of sunrises. Your strength is in your name; and power in the love you will have to take care of this family.

I bless you with wisdom to keep yourselves connected to each other; and never let anything in this life destroy the bonds of blood and brotherhood between you.

I bless you with the courage to face tomorrow without me; to be there for your mothers, sisters, wives and children; to show no fear when the world brings you to despair."

ACKNOWLEDGEMENTS

I am grateful to have been loved and cared for by many mothers.

In my grandmother's living room, there was a grandfather clock whose ticking sounded like people tilling the soil to my 5-year-old ears. Every time I was in there I would wonder why people were working so late in the night. How could they see the ground they were tilling and plant seeds?

One day I asked my grandmother why people were working through the night and she said it was the clock ticking. It blew my 5-year-old mind that a clock could sound like that and my grandmother was the most intelligent woman to have such a clock because I had not seen any other house with it. She was my first mother and teacher. I owe who I am to Ba Mbuya Ba Elina Chitundu for not only the generations of blood passed down but for scolding a naughty little Maswaswa as she called me and loving her unconditionally.

Mummy Leah, yours is the blood that runs through me and if am anything close to the woman you are then my life is complete. Natotela mayo wandi for your love, prayers and continued support.

This labour of love has been eight years in the making. I will definitely forget someone but let's see if I can say natotela sana to those who have been in my writing journey so far: Emily Gowor,

Anita Ojwang, Bojana, Kanyanta Chipanta, Samantha Jansen, Agnes Nsofwa, Christine Ampaire, Lisa Mangwiro, Kapesa Singogo, My one and only bolingo (you know yourself), Margaret Chikwibu, Mukuka Chipanta, Fiona Byarugaba, Richard Dove, Western Union Writers, Lina Singogo Millwood, George Mutale, Twaambo Kapilikisha, Helen Cerne, Amanda Green and last but not least my brother Katongo.

GLOSSARY

BOLINGO - Love in Lingala

CHALO - World

FRIDAY NJIKATA, SATURDAY NDEKELAKO, SUNDAY KU LONDOLOLA - Zambian saying for people who party all weekend long. Friday hold me tight, Saturday release me, Sunday go to church and explain your bad behaviour

MAYO - Mother

MU CHALO - In the world

NATOTELA - Thank you

NSHIMA (Zambia) - Also known as Ugali (Kenya/Uganda), Sadza (Zimbabwe), Tuwo (Nigeria), Pap (South Africa) - A staple food in parts of Africa. Cooked with mostly Maize/Corn meal or Cassava meal, Ground Millet or even Sorghum.

SANA - Very much

WANDI – Mine

ABOUT THE AUTHOR

Mayase Jere was born in Zambia and moved to Perth, Australia in 2004. She lives in Melbourne with her family.

Her passion is in empowering individuals to change their organisations through co-design, collaboration, rapid experimentation and increasing the participation of women leaders in Science, Technology, Engineering and Mathematics (STEM).

By day she is an Agile Product/Project Management practitioner who mentors individuals, coaches and leads software teams in developing platforms and digital products.

By night she is a co-founding member of Blacks in Tech Australia, a Podcaster/Blogger/Storyteller on The Art of Otherness and a Women in Tech Advocate.

Her first published short story was "Tram to Despair" part of the "Undefeated: 90 migrant women, 118 journeys" book anthology.

You can connect with her on Instagram @art_of_otherness